DISNEY'S
THE LITTLE
MERMAID

The Sunken Ship

DISNEY
PRESS

New York

Ariel stretched in her giant clamshell bed. "What a perfect day for exploring," she said to her friend Flounder.

Ariel had found some amazing things while searching the ocean caves and reefs. But most of her special treasures came from sunken ships. The ships were filled with trinkets from the human world—a world where Ariel longed to live.

"Come on," Ariel called to Flounder. "We have to find more shells for Alana's present." Ariel was making a shell necklace for her sister's birthday gift.

Soon the Little Mermaid spotted a row of beautiful shells. She picked them up one by one until she noticed she was right next to a sunken ship.

"Wow!" Ariel exclaimed. "Let's go inside. Maybe we'll find lots of treasure."

Inside, the ship was dark and eerily silent.

"There's s-s-something s-s-spooky about this ship," Flounder stammered.

"Oh, don't be such a guppy," Ariel said with a laugh. "I just know I'm going to find something special today."

Suddenly, they heard the most terrifying sound from somewhere inside the ship. *RUFFF! RUFFF! RUFFF!*

"I think it might be a monster!" cried Ariel.

Rushing out of the ship, Ariel and Flounder swam right into Sebastian the crab.

"Aaaah!" they all screamed.

Ariel began to tell Sebastian about the noise when all of a sudden, they heard it again. *RUFFF! RUFFF! RUFFF!*

"Let's get out of here!" Sebastian cried.

The friends quickly swam home.

That night, Ariel dreamed she was back in the ship with Flounder. They were being chased by a hideous monster.

"RUFFF! RUFFF! RUFFF!" cried the monster. Suddenly, it grabbed Flounder and swallowed him in one gulp. Next, the monster reached for Ariel.

"No!" screamed Ariel. "Leave me alone!"

"Ariel, wake up!" called King Triton. "You were having a nightmare."

The Little Mermaid told her father about her spooky dream and the scary sea monster.

"Only humans believe in monsters," King Triton said, trying to comfort her.

The next morning, Ariel told Flounder what she had planned for the day.

"We're going back to that ship," said Ariel, dragging Flounder along. "I left a bag of lovely shells in there."

"I think I'll w-w-wait out here," said Flounder, once they arrived at the ship.

Inside, Ariel soon spotted her bag. But before she could leave, she heard the terrifying sound again. *RUFFF! RUFFF! RUFFF!*

Monster or no monster, Ariel *had* to find out what was making that noise. She plunged deeper into the long, narrow ship. Trying not to think about the monster from her dream, she closed her eyes tightly.

When she opened her eyes, the monster was right in front of her! Only it wasn't a monster at all. It was something small and cute.

Ariel found Flounder, and they took the "monster" to Scuttle the seagull, who claimed to know all about the human world.

"This is a 'woofnhoofer,'" he said. "I saw a little girl playing with it on the beach. I think she's there now."

"Then we must return it to her," Ariel said.

And so, Scuttle dropped the "woofn-hoofer" on the beach near the little girl.

Ariel's heart melted as she watched the girl hug the toy dog. The Little Mermaid would never forget her adventure in the spooky ship and the special treasure she had discovered.